A Theodor Seuss Geisel Awa P9-DEY-545

A *New York Times Book Review* Best Illustrated
Children's Book of the Year

A *Publishers Weekly* Best Children's Book of the Year

A *Kirkus Reviews* Best Children's Book

• •

"Oh, happiness! Move over Pippi Longstocking. . . . Bink and Gollie . . .
join the ranks of George and Martha, Frog and Toad, Zelda and Ivy,
and all the other resilient pairs that celebrate the challenges and
strengths of a great friendship." —*The New York Times Book Review*

★ "If James Marshall's George and Martha were not hippos and were
both girls, they would be much like best friends Bink and Gollie. . . .
More, please!" —*Kirkus Reviews* (starred review)

★ "Think Pippi Longstocking meets *The Big Bang Theory*."
—*Publishers Weekly* (starred review)

• •

Bink & gollie

Kate DiCamillo and Alison McGhee

illustrated by Tony Fucile

CANDLEWICK PRESS

First paperback edition 2012

The Library of Congress has cataloged the hardcover edition as follows:

DiCamillo, Kate.
Bink and Gollie / Kate DiCamillo and Alison McGhee ; illustrated by Tony Fucile. — 1st ed.
p.   cm.
Summary: Two roller-skating best friends — one tiny, one tall — share
three comical adventures involving outrageously bright socks, an impromptu
trek to the Andes, and a most unlikely marvelous companion.
ISBN 978-0-7636-3266-3 (hardcover)
[1. Friendship — Fiction. 2. Adventure and adventurers — Fiction. 3. Humorous stories.]
I. McGhee, Alison, date. II. Fucile, Tony, ill. III. Title.
PZ7.D5455Bi 2010
[Fic] — dc22   2009049100

ISBN 978-0-7636-5954-7 (paperback)

15 16 17 18 CCP 10 9

Printed in Shenzhen, Guangdong, China

This book was typeset in Humana Sans.
The illustrations were done digitally.

Candlewick Press
99 Dover Street
Somerville, Massachusetts 02144

visit us at www.candlewick.com

For Karla Marie Rydrych, friend of my heart

K. D.

To Cindy Schultz Sykes, marvelous companion of my youth

A. M.

To Karen and Nina

T. F.

Contents

Don't You Need a New Pair of Socks?

2

P. S. I'll Be Back Soon
●
26

Give a Fish a Home
●
46

Don't You Need a New Pair of Socks?

"Hello, Gollie," said Bink.

"What should we do today?"

"Greetings, Bink," said Gollie.

"I long for speed."

"Let's roller-skate!"

"I do need a new pair of socks!" said Bink. "Let's go inside."

"Hello," said Bink. "I'm here for the socks."

"It's a sock bonanza!" said Bink.

"Indeed it is," said Gollie. "An extremely bright sock bonanza."

SOCK SALE

"I'll take this pair,"
said Bink.

"Bink," said Gollie, "the brightness
of those socks pains me. I beg
you not to purchase them."

"I can't wait to put
them on," said Bink.

"I love socks," said Bink.
"Some socks are more lovable
than others," said Gollie.

"I especially love bright socks," said Bink.

"Putting on socks is hard work," said Bink. "I'm hungry."

"Maybe Gollie is making pancakes."

"Hello, Gollie," said Bink.
"Do I smell pancakes?"
"You do not," said Gollie.
"Will I smell pancakes?"
said Bink.

"Perhaps a compromise is in order, Bink," said Gollie.

"What's a compromise?" said Bink.

"Use your gray matter, Bink," said Gollie. "You remove your outrageous socks, and I will make pancakes."

"The problem with Gollie," said Bink, "is that it's either Gollie's way or the highway."

"My socks and I have chosen the highway."

"The problem with Bink," said Gollie, "is her unwillingness to compromise."

"Greetings, Bink," said Gollie. "I am eating pancakes. What are you doing?"

"I'm wearing my socks," said Bink.

"I have brought you half of my pancakes," said Gollie.

"And I've removed one of my outrageous socks," said Bink. "It's a compromise bonanza!"

P.S.

I'll

Be

Back

Soon

"It has been far too long since my last adventure,"
said Gollie. "I must journey forth into the wider
world. But where?

"Tasmania? Timbuktu?"

"The finger has spoken," said Gollie.

"I'm baffled," said Bink.
"Am I 'whom'?"

KNOCK,
KNOCK,
KNOCK!

"I cannot talk right now," said Gollie.

"Why not?" said Bink.

"Because," said Gollie, "I am high in the
pure air of the Andes Mountains."

"All righty, then,"
said Bink.

"I wonder if Gollie's home yet," said Bink.

"Hmm," said Bink.

KNOCK,
KNOCK,
KNOCK!

"Please," said Gollie. "Have you not read the sign?"

"I read it," said Bink. "Aren't you hungry?"

"Not at all," said Gollie.

"Not even a little?" said Bink.

"Not even a little," said Gollie.

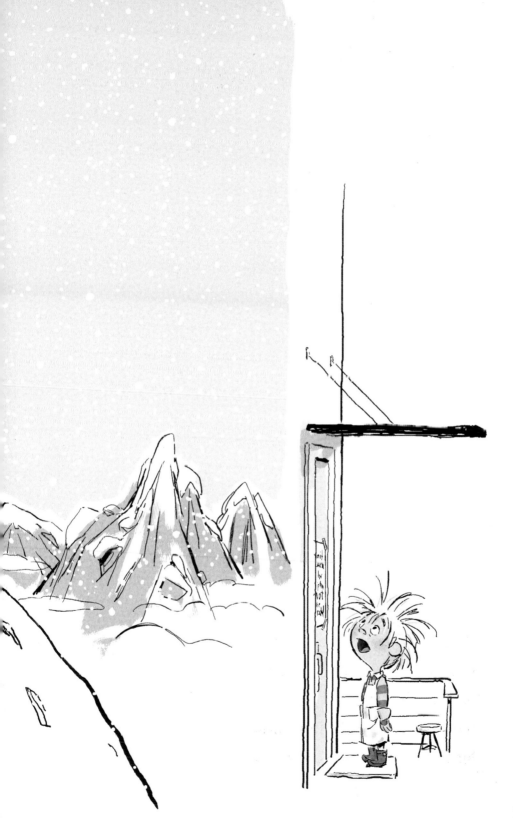

"Not even a bit
hungry!" said Bink.

"I don't believe it."

"What does *implore* mean?" said Bink.

**KNOCK,
KNOCK,
KNOCK!**

"Bink," said Gollie, "you must let me journey."

"But I brought you a sandwich," said Bink.

"Here I am," said Gollie, "where none but a few have ventured. What an extraordinary accomplishment."

"Bink!" said Gollie. "Come see."

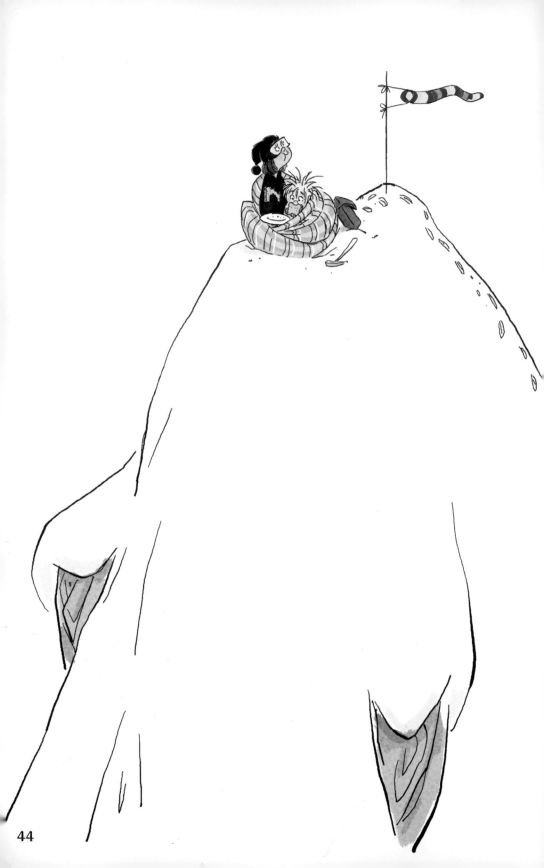

Give

a

Fish

a

Home

"As you can see," said Mr. Fishman, "these are truly remarkable fish. Spectacular in virtually every way. Marvelous companions, marvelous. Each one desperate for a good home."

"I'll take that one," said Bink.

"Bink," said Gollie, "I must inform you that you are
giving a home to a truly unremarkable fish."
"I love him," said Bink.

"Furthermore," said Gollie, "that fish is incapable
of being a marvelous companion."
"I wonder what his name is," said Bink.

"Greetings, Bink," said Gollie. "Would you like to join me for pancakes?"

"Fred and I are on our way," said Bink.

"I only made enough pancakes for two," said Gollie.

"Fred can share with me," said Bink.

"I only have two chairs," said Gollie.

"Oh, Fred doesn't need a chair," said Bink.

"Gollie, do you want to go see *Mysteries of the Deep Blue Sea*?" said Bink.

"Is that the movie about the fish?" said Gollie.

"It is!" said Bink. "It's the movie about the fish."

"Fred thinks that was a top-quality fish film."
said Bink.

"I'm not sure I agree," said Gollie.

"Fred has a great idea," said Bink.

"I am almost afraid to inquire," said Gollie.

"Fred wants to roller-skate," said Bink. "Fred longs for speed."

"Fish know nothing of longing," said Gollie.

"Some fish do," said Bink. "Some fish long."

"Hey!" said Bink. "Wait up for me and Fred!"

"Don't be afraid, Fred," said Bink.

"Oh, no," said Bink.

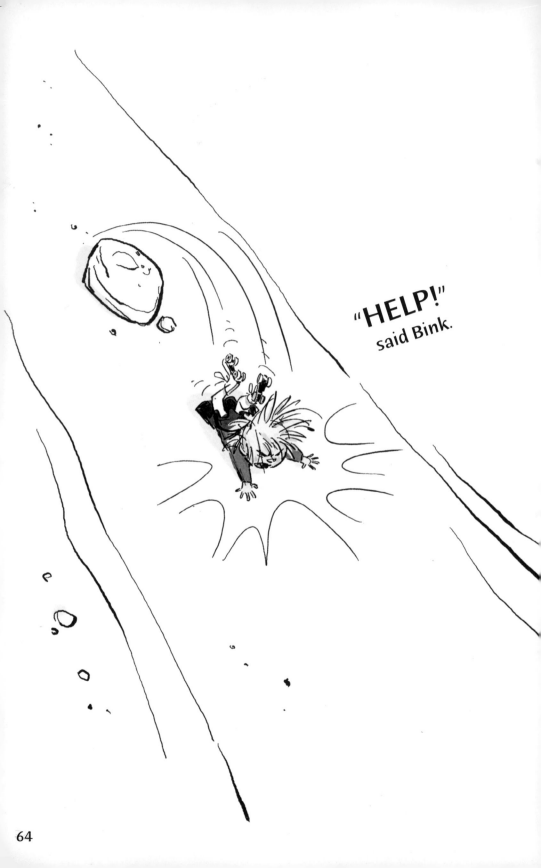

"HELP!"
said Bink.

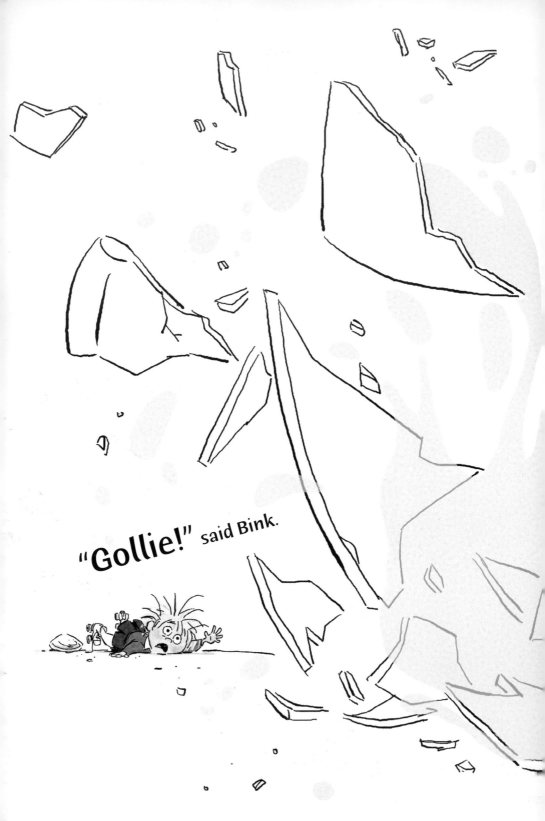

"Gollie!" said Bink.

"What are you doing?"

"Step aside," said Gollie.

"Wait!" said Bink. "Where are you going?"

"Help! Give me back my fish!"

"What have you done
with Fred?" said Bink.

"I have saved Fred's life," said Gollie.

"How can Fred be my marvelous companion if he's in the pond?" said Bink.

"You can come and visit him," said Gollie. "If you feel the need of a marvelous companion."

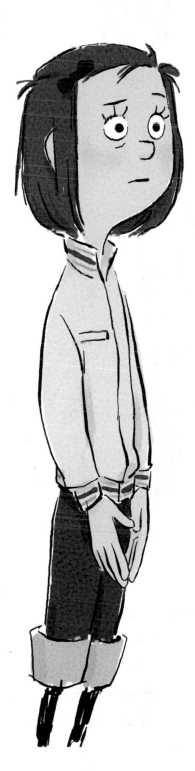

"I think you're jealous
of Fred," said Bink.

"Gollie," said Bink, "use your gray matter. Don't you know that you are the most marvelous companion of all?"

"Really?" said Gollie.

"Really," said Bink.

Six months later . . .

Kate DiCamillo is the author of many books for young readers, including *Flora & Ulysses: The Illuminated Adventures* and *The Tale of Despereaux*, both of which won Newbery Medals; six books starring Mercy Watson; and the Mercy spin-off series, Tales from Deckawoo Drive. In 2014 she was named the National Ambassador for Young People's Literature. She lives in Minneapolis.

Alison McGhee is the author of several picture books, including *Song of Middle C*, illustrated by Scott Menchin, and the #1 *New York Times* bestseller *Someday*, illustrated by Peter H. Reynolds; novels for children and young adults, including *All Rivers Flow to the Sea* and the Julia Gillian series; and several novels for adults, including the best-selling *Shadow Baby*, which was a *Today* Book Club selection and was nominated for a Pulitzer Prize. She lives in Minnesota and Vermont.

Tony Fucile is the author-illustrator of *Let's Do Nothing!* and the illustrator of *Mitchell's License* by Hallie Durand. He has spent more than twenty years designing and animating characters for numerous feature films, including *The Lion King*, *Finding Nemo*, and *The Incredibles*. He lives in the San Francisco Bay area.

Look out for *Bink & Gollie: Two for One* and *Bink & Gollie: Best Friends Forever*!

To learn more about the series and its creators, visit www.binkandgollie.com